Lovestruck at Swindlemore Hall

Other plays by the same author in English

An innocent little murder

Casket for two

Cheaters

Crisis and Punishment

Critical but stable

Friday the 13th

Him and Her

Quarantine

Running on Empty

Strip Poker

The Worst Village in England

JEAN-PIERRE MARTINEZ

Lovestruck at Swindlemore Hall

English translation by
Anne-Christine Gasc

La Comédiathèque
comediatheque.net

Characters

Carlota, Baroness Swindlemore von Hustlestein
Marika, her daughter
Marina, her maid
Frank, her son-in-law

ISBN 978-2-37705-795-5

Act 1

The living room of Swindlemore Hall, dilapidated and furnished with valuable genuine antiques but in a pitiful state. A few family portraits hung askew barely hiding the decaying state of the walls. Marika Swindlemore von Hustlestein enters, frumpy and ungainly.

Marika – Marina? Where did this halfwit go? Marina! Unbelievable!

Her mother Carlota, Baroness Swindlemore von Hustlestein, enters. A rather voluptuous woman, she is wearing a lot of makeup and is dressed with a flashy elegance. She is carrying a breakfast tray.

Marika – Oh, hello Mother ... Might you have seen the maid?

Carlota – She just left ...

Marika – Left? To go where? When might she be back?

Carlota – Not anytime soon, I'm afraid ...

Marika – How do you mean? I need her now! (*Having doubts*) Don't tell me she took off for another vacation in … wherever she's from?

Carlota – If only ...

Marika – Do you mean she just took off?

Carlota – That is unfortunately what happens when staff wages are not paid ...

Marika – These people really have no manners ... She could've at least brought me my breakfast before leaving … Oh well, plenty more fish in the sea ... She never could manage to soft-boil an egg anyway ...

The baroness places the tray on a table.

Carlota – Well, today, as a treat, I made your soft-boiled egg myself ... Happy birthday darling!

Marika – You remembered! What a treasure you are, Mother dear ...

Carlota – Your present will have to wait a little. I'm sure you're aware of our small cash flow issues ...

Marika sits up and starts on the soft-boiled egg.

Marika – Don't torment yourself, Mother. And yours is perfection! Bravo!

Carlota – Mine?

Marika – Your soft-boiled egg!

Carlota – Oh right, of course ... Well, if our finances continue their current downwards trend, I could always take a housekeeping job in one of the neighbouring manors ...

Marika – You're so funny, Mother.

Carlota – I hired a replacement for the maid, but we can't afford to pay her either so she probably won't stay much longer than the one who just left ...

Marika – Is everything all right, Mother? You seem concerned. Don't worry about Marina. I can do without a chambermaid for a day or two.

Carlota – Marika, we need to have a talk.

Marika – You're frightening me ... It looks very serious indeed ... But proceed, I am listening ...

Carlota – Marika, you are no longer a child. You are now able to understand certain things ... As you've come to realise since you came home from Wycombe Abbey, our financial situation is a most delicate affair. We cannot afford to pay the staff and the manor is falling apart.

Marika – Actually, I wanted to talk to you about that. Do you know that famous line from Shakespeare: "Here comes the rain again, falling on my head like a memory"?

Carlota – I believe it is from Eurythmics.

Marika – Whatever, in my case it's a literal description of what's happening in my bedroom.

Carlota – Well Marika, I may have found a way to permanently fix the holes in our cashflow and to restore this manor before it finally collapses on our heads.

Marika – Are you thinking of those games of luck advertised by the National Lottery on the radio, who would turn a peasant into a lord with a few brightly colored balls?

Carlota – I was thinking of a different kind of balls, my dear child. Ones that are part of the game of love, rather than games of chance. Believe me, the odds are much better ...

Marika – I'm afraid I don't follow ...

Carlota – Given your age, it is time for you to find a husband… Have you put any thought into it?

Marika – Well ...

Carlota – I know, nowadays it's not that easy for a young woman from a good family to find a suitor worth their salt. Especially when one sets the bar a little high. Baroness Swindlemore von Hustlestein's daughter can't marry just anyone.

Marika – Absolutely.

Carlota – One day, you will inherit my baroness title. Actually, I fear that the way things are going, that's the only thing I will be able to leave you ...

Marika – Come, come ... We're not there yet ... And anyhow, as you say so yourself, nowadays prince charmings are not exactly queuing out the door ...

Carlota – And that is precisely why in this matter, a mother's discrete intervention might come in handy ...

Marika – Really?

Carlota – A mother ... and a little help from these newfangled communication technologies, of course ...

Marika – Did you register my profile on one of those dating websites without telling me?

Carlota – A very exclusive dating website, I assure you. I even had to increase your potential dowry and Photoshop your picture a little bit ...

Marika – My picture?

Carlota – Thankfully, your name itself is a fixed value capital. Many high-net-worth individuals would be flattered to marry a baroness Swindlemore, even one without a penny to her name ... purely for the respectability it carries, that money could never buy.

Marika – But Mother ... You would marry me to a commoner?

Carlota – Alas, we must face reality, my dear child. People of our class are just as skint as we are ...

Marika – There's being skint and there's pimping your daughter to a nouveau riche to regain some standing ...

Carlota – Unfortunately, I don't see any other solution ... I googled "adopting a noble dot com" but nothing came up ... Believe me, we have no choice ...

Marika – Couldn't we just sell something?

Carlota – I already sold everything we could, I assure you ... It's either that or we sell off Swindlemore Hall. The family seat for seven generations ...

Marika – But I don't want to leave you, Mother!

Carlota – You could live here with your husband. The manor is big enough. We'll just have to find a man who isn't too picky… and as rich as he is easily pleased ...

Marika – Well… Why not, after all? We never entertain. It might be a hoot to meet with a few suitors. We can judge them in the flesh ...

Carlota – Your 9 o'clock will be here any minute now.

Marika – My 9 o'clock? You sound like a medical secretary! Announcing a patient for a root canal! Next, you'll be telling me the waiting room is full.

Carlota – Don't worry, he's the only one suitor to date. And it wasn't easy to find him either ...

Marika – But Mother, I haven't even brushed my hair!

Carlota – I shouldn't worry, it won't be a problem.

Marika – How so?

Carlota – I mean, you're perfect the way you are, dear.

Marika – Can you at least tell me what this young man is like?

Carlota – He's the only heir to a real estate mogul, originally from Wales, who made his fortune in California.

Marika – I meant ... physically.

The doorbell rings.

Carlota – Sounds like you'll be able to see for yourself …

Marika – Oh my God! But you should have given me more notice!

Carlota – I wasn't sure how you'd react. I thought it best to keep it a surprise. Right, I'll go let him in myself. Not having a maid anymore and all ...

Carlota leaves. Marika seems both worried and excited. She tries to straighten her hair a little. But her mother returns immediately, followed by the newcomer.

Carlota – Come in, come in. Please ignore the mess, the maid has the day off ...

The suitor enters. He is wearing a dark suit, dark glasses and uses a white cane to find his way. He is holding a bouquet of flowers. Marika is stunned speechless.

Carlota – Marika, this is Mr Stonedef.

Frank – Hello Marika.

Marika – How do you do ...?

Frank moves towards her, holding out his bouquet of flowers. He trips on a small side table and a vase tips over. Marika remains stunned for a few seconds.

Frank – Please, call me Frank.

Marika takes Frank's bouquet while her mother picks up the vase.

Marika – Welcome to Swindlemore Hall, Frank ...

Carlota – Oh, just look at those flowers, you shouldn't have ... They are really gorgeous ... Aren't they Marika?

Marika – Yes, gorgeous ... Thank you very much ...

Carlota – We'll put them in a vase right away ...

Carlota picks up the fallen vase off the ground and Marika drops the flowers inside.

Carlota – There ... May I offer you a refreshment, Mr Stonedef? A tea or perhaps a coffee? I've never made any myself, but I'm sure I can have a go ...

Frank – Thank you, I'm good ... I came straight from LA. I had breakfast on the plane.

Carlota – My daughter was so keen to meet you ... I imagine you'll be staying a few days in France ...

Frank – Well ... I was hoping to stay sort of indefinitely … But that kind of depends on your daughter, actually ...

Marika looks like she is made of stone.

Carlota – She's a little shy, you know ... She was educated in an abbey… Well, I mean, she wasn't a nun, let me assure you.

Frank – No worries, I have no intention of rushing things.

Carlota – She studied at Wycombe Abbey, you know. Just like Mary Pickford.

Frank – They didn't graduate in the same year, I hope.

Carlota *(laughing loudly)* – You're so funny ... Isn't he hilarious, dear? *(Marika is still frozen)* Of course it's a little difficult for you to judge, but believe me: Marika is an absolutely lovely young woman ...

Frank – I believe you Baroness. Anyway, don't they say that love is blind?

Carlota *(laughing again)* – You're such a hoot! But say something, Marika. Or Mr Stonedef will think you're mute.

Marika – You ... I mean how ...?

Carlota – My daughter is trying to ask you how you came to be ... Were you born that way, or ...

Frank – Well ... Truth be told ... I was struck by lighting when I was 18 years old.

Carlota – Struck by lighting ... My God, how exciting. Isn't it, dear?

Frank – Take my word for it, if you ever end up in the countryside during a thunderstorm, don't seek shelter under one of those metal crucifixes that you find at some crossroads.

Marika – Why ever not?

Frank – But because it attracts lighting, Miss.

Carlota – Crucifixes make perfect lighting rods, it's well known.

Frank – Sometimes I feel like it's our Lord himself that sent me this hardship, to atone for all my sins ...

Carlota – So you believe in God ...

Frank – Faith is one of the few comforts I have in this world ...

Carlota – I personally insisted that my daughter be brought up according to the principles of the Holy Catholic Roman church ...

Frank – Listen, Marika, I won't beat around the bush because I'm running out of time. I know I don't have much going for me, apart from my honest intentions and my enormous fortune.

Carlota – Which is very important to us, rest assured, Mr Stonedef ... I mean, the part about your honest intentions, of course ...

Frank – Enormous fortune that I will lay at the feet of my future wife ... The one who will be able to see the deep need for love that is hidden behind these dark glasses ...

Carlota – What is it they say ... Eyes are the windows to the soul! Unfortunately, in your case the shutters are closed. But I have a feeling you'll soon find someone to pry them open and let fresh air into this house ...

Frank – Marika, along with your name, you have inherited the nobility and grace befitting your title. And you have received a decent education. I am looking to marry a young woman who isn't interested in my money and will be my guide in life. And you must understand that in my state, gentleness and kindness are more important than physical perfection ...

Carlota – That's great to hear, Mr Stonedef. *(Marika glares at her mother)* I mean, that's very noble of you, Frank. My daughter, as you know, will one day inherit the title of Baroness of Swindlemore ... A lineage that, as you can see by the family portraits here, has a track record of shining through British history ...

Marika – Mother ...

Carlota – Please pardon me, I forgot that ...

Frank – No worries, Madam.

Carlota – Please, call me Carlota.

Frank – But why?

Carlota – Well, because that's my name!

Frank – I was joking, Madam. I mean, Carlota.

Carlota – You're unbelievable! Isn't he, dear? I would have never thought that a cripple could be so funny ... I mean ...

The doorbell rings.

Carlota – Please excuse me, that must be the new maid of honor ... I mean the new maid ...

Frank – Oh, I thought you said your housekeeper just had the day off ...

Carlota – That's true, and that's the very reason why I decided to get rid of her ... She was taking too many days off ... You know what it's like, they all want to work a 4-day week ... I'll leave you for just a moment. Why don't you use this time to get acquainted ...?

Carlota leaves. Marika remains alone with Frank, not really knowing what to say.

Frank – Anyway, you have a lovely voice ...

Marika – Thank you ...

Another silence.

Frank – It would give me great pleasure to hear it more… You can ask me questions, you know. That way we could get to know one another ...

Marika – I don't know, I ... Do you play the piano?

Frank – Er, no .... Why do you ask?

Marika is embarrassed.

Marika – Excuse me, I need to have a word with my mother ...

Marika leaves. Frank watches her leave, without her noticing. He removes his dark glasses, looks around and is not impressed by the shabby furniture. He looks closely at the paintings and seems more satisfied. Carlota and Marika return with the new maid. Frank puts his dark glasses back on.

Carlota – My apologies for leaving you alone ... This is Marina, our new maid ...

Marika – Her name is Marina too?

Carlota – Yes, just like the one we let go. It's rather convenient, isn't it?

Marina – Oi, I got soaked through my knickers cutting across the park.

Marina, a young woman charmingly vulgar, walks towards Frank.

Carlota – I have noticed that around half of the maids I know are called Marina. I wonder why that is ...

Marina – Sir ...

Frank – Madam ...

Marina – Miss ... Well, you're an optimist aren't you! With them dark glasses ... Expecting sunshine in this weather…!

She holds out her hand to Frank who pretends to not see it. Carlota and Marika exchange dismayed looks.

Carlota – Please excuse her ... It's so hard to find staff these days ... Marina, why don't you go see what's going on in the pantry? We'll call for you later…

Marina – Yes, Madam ...

Carlota – Just a thought, now that we have found another maid, might Mr Stonedef now like a proper cup of tea? Just between us, God knows Eastern European maids aren't perfect, but they do brew the most delicious tea ...

Frank – Don't bother on my behalf ... Actually, I'll be on my way ...

Carlota – Are you leaving us already, Mr Stonedef?

Frank sneezes.

Frank – Excuse me, I'm allergic to pollen ... It must be the flowers I brought ...

Marina – Are you sure it's not the dust, more like? *(Marina looks around the room)* Looks like the dust bunnies have been going at it for a while ... know what I mean? You'd have to be blind to not see it, right Mr Stonedef?

Frank – I have to go, but I'll be back soon ... Marika, it was lovely to meet you ...

Marika – Same here, Frank.

Frank – My friends call me Franky ...

Marika – Goodbye Franky.

Carlota – My daughter will walk you out ... Won't you dear?

Frank picks up his white cane and gets out of his chair. Marina understands that he is blind.

Marina – Oh right ... Sorry Mr Stonedef, I didn't see you were blind, like.

Frank – Don't worry about it, it happens a lot.

Marina – It's okay, I don't mind cripples, me. Actually, I find that scandalous, these people who park in those handicapped places they save for blind folks in car parks, don't you?

The baroness and her daughter exchange a look, aghast.

Carlota – We hope to see you again very soon, Frank.

Frank – Thank you for your delightful hospitality, Baroness.

Marika leaves with Frank on her arm.

Marina – So, you're a baroness then?

Carlota – Indeed. I am Baroness of Swindlemore von Hustlestein. The seventh.

Marina – Wow ... I've never seen a baroness before.

Carlota – Well, now that you've seen me maybe you can get on with your work, what do you think? What's your name again?

Marina – Marina.

Carlota – That's right. Well, Marina, how about starting by removing this tray and then moving on to a bit of house cleaning?

Marika returns. Marina stares at her.

Marina – You're my mother's doppelganger.

Carlota – Thank you for not saying that in front of her suitor ... Speaking of which, in the future I would ask that you refrain from speaking to our guests, is that understood? So, Marika, what do you think?

Marina – It's uncanny. And we have the same name!

Marika – Er ... Not quite ... I'm Marika.

Marina – Oh sorry, I thought you said Marina. Still, you look so much like her, it's crazy. It's like we're related.

Marika – What is your mother's patronym?

Marina – Her what?

Carlota – Her surname!

Marina – Yvanov, like me.

Carlota – In that case, it's unlikely that we are related. In fact, the family branch that was related to the Russian royal family died under the revolution ...

Marina – Russian? But I'm not Russian.

Marika – You're not Russian?

Marina – Well no, I'm from Belarus.

Carlota – Yes, well, same thing ...

Marina – Oh no, it's not the same thing at all. Speaking of which, do you know what Marika means in my language?

Carlota – No, and no one cares, believe it or not.

Marina – Well, I wouldn't want to be called Marika ...

Carlota – How about you take this tray and see what's going on in the kitchen?

Marina – Very well, Madam the baroness. *(Marina leaves, roaring with laughter)* Marika ... It means 'bitter' … Fitting ... Bitter by name, bitter by nature ...!

The others watch her leave with dismayed looks.

Carlota – So? What do you think?

Marika – About what? The new maid?

Carlota – Your suitor! I thought it went rather well, didn't you?

Marika *(exploding)* – Rather well? He's blind and he doesn't even play the piano!

Carlota – Alright, he may not be the ideal husband ... But from a financial point of view, he's the ideal son-in-law. He's a billionaire! He's the solution to all our problems!

Marika – Sounds like you should marry him ...

Carlota – He might be visually impaired, but he would still notice I'm old enough to be his mother. We don't have a choice, dear, we really don't. It's either that or we start cooking and cleaning for ourselves. Because that new maid of ours, we're going to have to pay her if we want her to stay.

Marika – We can always sell a few more pieces of furniture ...

Carlota – If we sell any more we'll have to sit on the floor ... You have to be blind to ignore the state of this manor…

Marika – What about the family portraits?

Carlota – Never!

Marika – Oh, but selling me isn't a problem?

Carlota – Come, come Marika, you're not a child anymore ... Don't tell me you're still waiting for Prince Charming ... Remember, you don't have to love your husband! And should you decide to take a lover, well, being married to a blind man could be an advantage.

Marika – You have an interesting concept of marriage, mother ...

Carlota – The only thing he's expecting in exchange for the millions he will lay at your feet is a little company and someone to guide him through life.

Marika – Mother, please ... I'm not a guide dog!

Carlota – I'm sure you could learn to bark in no time ... I'm teasing. We certainly could use a healthy graft to revive our stunted family tree ...

Marika – A healthy graft? This cripple?

Carlota – It would also revive our bank account ...

Marika – No really, mother. You can't expect me to sacrifice this much ...

Carlota – I would ask that you take a bit of time to think before making your decision, dear ... Be reasonable ... Consider that it might be difficult to marry you off with someone more ... discerning… Speaking of which, he hasn't proposed yet ...

Marika – A blind fiancé… I expected a little better for my birthday ...

Marina returns with a feather duster to tackle the furniture.

Marina – It's your birthday, Miss Marika?

Marika – Yes, why? Do you have a gift for me too?

Marina – That's unbelievable!

Marika – What now?

Marina – It's my birthday too! I'm twenty years old today. You?

Marika – Me too.

Marina – And we're born the same day!

Carlota – Yes, well ... Several million people in the world are born on this day. Not that unbelievable.

Marina – In the world maybe, but in the UK.

Carlota – I thought you were born in Belarus?

Marina – My father and mother are from Belarus. I was born in Essex, in Sodgibbon.

Marika – No …? Sodgibbon ...?

Marina – Don't tell me ...

Carlota – That is a strange coincidence. But several people were also born in the maternity ward of Sodgibbon on that day.

Marina – Not people that look just like my mother! Look, I have a photo!

Marina pulls a photo from her pocket and holds it to Marika's face, who looks at it carefully, troubled.

Marika – Ah yes ... There is a certain… family resemblance ...

Carlota – Right, Marina, how about you went and cleaned the bedrooms now?

Marina – Very well Madam Baroness. But you can't stop me thinking this is all very unusual ...

Marina leaves without taking her photo with her.

Carlota – I wonder if we shouldn't let this one go right now ...

Marika – You have to admit, this story is quite troubling …

Carlota – Oh, not you as well!

Marika holds the photo to her mother.

Marika – Don't you think the resemblance is striking?

Carlota – Oh please, can't you see the poor girl is completely out of her mind! How could someone of your standing look like an Eastern European maid or her mother?

Marika – It's a fact that I look nothing like you.

Carlota – Children don't always look like their parents. What is your point?

Marika – These things happen. It was in a film. Two children who accidentally get switched at birth in the hospital ...

Carlota – Sometimes air traffic controllers send storks the wrong way ...

Marika – I remember ... The blue-blood one ends up in a council flat in Tower Hamlets, while the chav one ends up in Kensington.

Carlota – You watch too much television, dear… This is preposterous. According to your theory, I would be the maid's mother? Do you think we look alike?

Marika – No, of course not ...

Carlota – Well, there you go!

Marika – Still ...You know that mole on the left buttock, the Swindlemore trademark ... You have it, I don't. What I have is a hairy back ...

Carlota – Genetic lottery. Sometimes it can skip a generation. It's like genius and beauty. Apparently, Einstein's son was an idiot, and who knows, if Marilyn had had a child, she might have had a face like a dropped pie.

Marika *(lost in thought)* – Still ... I'd quite like a peek at the maid's buttocks ...

Carlota appears disconcerted for a moment. The doorbell rings.

Carlota *(distracted)* – Who might that be at this time of day?

Marika – Why, what time is it?

Carlota – I don't know, I don't know why I said that ...

The maid returns, guiding Frank by the arm.

Marina – Mr Stonedef left his gloves ...

Frank – That's true, but I have to admit there's another reason for returning so soon ...

Marina is waiting, visibly eager to find out more.

Carlota – Thank you Marina, that will be all ...

Marina – Very well Madam Baroness.

Marina leaves reluctantly.

Frank – Is your daughter present?

Marika motions that no, she isn't.

Carlota – Do you wish for me to call her ...?

Marika is about to leave the room discretely, but Frank steps forward and stands in her way.

Frank – Actually, I think it would be best if I confided in you instead ...

Carlota – Confide...? Are you looking for absolution?

Frank – It's a little embarrassing but ... well ... I didn't tell you the whole truth earlier ...

Frank – You're not the billionaire you pretend to be?

Frank – No, no, don't worry, it's nothing like that. It's about the cause of my blindness.

Carlota – Oh thank God ... I mean ... The cause of your …

Frank – Earlier I told you that I had been struck by lightning ... In truth, that's not how I lost my sight ...

Carlota – We are all a little vain, dearest Frank. You don't have to explain to a woman how cute lies can be used to improve the truth a little ...

Frank – The reason for my disability is, alas, a lot more pedestrian. I have an incurable disease ...

Carlota – Incurable ... As in, there is no cure ...? No cure at all…?

Frank – Yes, that is indeed what I mean when I say it is incurable.

Carlota – But incurable doesn't necessarily imply that it's terminal ...

Frank – Unfortunately, in my case it does. A year ago I was diagnosed with a brain tumor in a location affecting the optic nerve. Alas, the tumor will continue to grow and affect other functions ... The doctors think I will be gone within six months ...

Carlota – But that's horrible…! I'm so sorry ... But ... Why are you telling me? I'm not a doctor ...

Frank – It's like this. I am going to die without an heir. That's also why I want to get married very quickly. So I don't have to die alone. And also to have someone to leave my fortune to after my death. Rather than see it end up donated to a useless charity or claimed by the taxman …

Carlota *(regaining hope)* – That's a very wise decision, Mr Stonedef ... And very generous too, if I may say so ...

Frank – I know that my proposal will seem rushed, but now you'll understand why ... I would like to know whether you would give me your blessing to ask for your daughter's hand in marriage. I was very taken by her, earlier. And you too, of course. I felt I had found a family, and a home, as soon as I entered your manor ...

Carlota and Marika exchange an awkward look.

Carlota – Yes, well, indeed ... This is all rather sudden … Looks like love at first sight ... I'm sorry, I keep forgetting that ...

Frank – Don't worry about it ...

Carlota – Listen, it will be up to my daughter of course, but ... As far as I'm concerned, if she agrees, you have my blessing ...

Frank – I am deeply grateful for your support, Madam. In that case, I'll disappear ...

Carlota – You'll disappear…?

Frank – I mean, I'll make myself scarce … Temporarily.

Carlota – Oh, of course. But what about your gloves?

Frank – I don't wear gloves ... We'll see each other very soon, Madam Baroness ...

He tries to leave using his cane as a guide but walks into the side table again, tipping over the vase and flowers.

Carlota – Please, wait a moment ... Marina!

Marina, who was obviously hiding behind the door, appears immediately.

Marina – Yes, Madam Baroness?

Carlota – Please show Mr Stonedef the way out ...

Marina – Very well, Madam.

Carlota – We hope to see you again very soon, Mr Stonedef. *(Frank leaves, guided my Marina.)* This time we're backed into a corner ...

Marika – It's a nightmare.

Carlota – This guy is a billionaire ... in US dollars! And he's only got a few months left to live… It's not a nightmare, it's a miracle! It's like playing the lottery, but with much better odds.

Marika – I was talking about the uncertainty about my birth! I could marry this man and the next day find out I am Mrs Kalashnikoff's daughter.

Carlota – Didn't she say her name was Romanoff?

Marika – How is that better?

Carlota – It's not. But there's no evidence that you're related to her. So, what do you want to do about Frank, dear?

Marika – I need to know for sure before committing one way or the other.

Carlota – Know for sure? But how?

The maid returns.

Marina – Can I start on the dusting?

Carlota – Sure, go ahead ...

The maid starts dusting the room with a feather duster. Marika stares at her to the point where the maid is a little uncomfortable.

Marika – Marina, why don't you go to the pantry and put on the uniform that the maid before you left behind.

Marina – A uniform?

Marika – You know ... Black dress, small white apron, headdress ...

Carlota – Have you ever watched *Benny Hill?*

Marina – I haven't, Madam.

Marika – We're sticklers for tradition around here, and we insist that a maid looks like a maid.

Marina – Very well, Miss.

Marika – So, go!

Marina – Right now?

Marika – Right now.

Marina – Very well, Miss.

The maid leaves.

Carlota – You should have told her to wax her facial hair as well ...

Marika – It's horrible ...

Carlota – I agree. So much more noticeable than a hairy back.

Marika – Can you imagine? If we were actually switched at birth, I would be the maid and Marina would be ... your daughter.

Carlota – Come now ... Stop torturing yourself! It's all poppycock! You don't speak Belarussian, do you?

Marika – No.

Carlota – Well, there you go! And the natural grace that people of our class inherit with our genes ... You can't fake that, I should know. You can plainly see that this wench doesn't carry herself the way a baroness of Swindlemore would.

Marika – Still ... I won't be able to let it go until I check for myself ...

Marika leaves the room. The baroness is alone and sighs. The phone rings and she picks up.

Carlota – Carlota Swindlemore von Hustlestein speaking. Yes ... Yes, yes, I know ... I can assure you this very small overdraft will soon be taken care of. How much? Oh, I see ... Listen, we are expecting some income and ... What's the point of a credit union if we can't count on the support of more fortunate clients to ...? Very well ... And as a last resort we can always sell a few paintings ... Understood, leave it with me and I'll call you back ...

She hangs up, visibly preoccupied. She starts to pick up the vase and the flowers that Frank knocked off the table when he left. Marika returns.

Marika – The maid has a mole on the lower part of her butt cheek ...

Carlota – I beg your pardon?

Marika – I was in the pantry when she was putting on her French maid's outfit. To check.

Carlota – Which buttock?

Marika – The left.

Carlota – Well then! The Swindlemores have it on the right buttock.

Marika – But earlier you told me it could skip a generation! Maybe it can also skip to the other buttock!

Carlota – Marika, please ...

Marika – Me, the daughter of Mrs Smirnoff ...

Carlota – How can you even imagine such a thing?

Marika – I think I'm going to be sick ...

Marika leaves and passes the maid who is returning, wearing a French maid's outfit.

Marina – The last time I saw this kind of uniform it was on a pay-per-view channel and it wasn't *Benny Hill* ...

Carlota – Oh yes ...

Marina – And your daughter Marika, she seems a little …

Carlota – A little what?

Marina – She walked in on me as I was putting this thing on and stared at my bottom ...

Marika returns.

Marina – Are you ok Miss Marika? You're very pale ...

Marika – I'll be fine.

Marina – Still, it's unbelievable how much you look like my mother ...

Marika feels faint again.

Carlota – That will be all Marina, thank you ...

The maid leaves.

Marika – Mother ... You wouldn't be hiding something from me, would you?

Carlota – But of course not, dear! Why would you even say something like that?

Marika – When you gave birth, do you remember if there was another baby there called Marina?

Carlota – How would I know! The babies were all lined up in a row in their basinets, like caged chickens ... I remember they placed you under a lamp because you had jaundice. Turns out your skin never really lost that yellow tint.

Marika – Thanks ...

Carlota – How do you even tell one baby from another? A mistake could easily happen ...

Marika – That's reassuring ...

Carlota – That's why they put bracelets on them!

Marika – Like an electronic bracelet?

Carlota – Not back then, no. Just a bracelet with the baby's name.

Marika – Unbelievable. Cars have license plates, VIN numbers on the chassis and the windshield, all sorts of anti-theft markings, and that's before we even get to various car alarm systems... But for a baby it's just a bracelet with a name on it, when nothing looks more like a baby than another baby.

Carlota – Especially since there's only one letter difference between Marika and Marina. If the baby gnaws on their bracelet at just the right place ...

Marika – Did you keep it? My bracelet?

Carlota – Of course not ... whatever for?

Marika – I don't know ... As a souvenir ...

The maid return, very excited.

Marina – I knew it, I was right!

Carlota – What now?

Marina – I just had my mother on the phone.

Marika – So what?

Marina – She admitted she always thought I wasn't her biological daughter.

Carlota – So why didn't she say anything?

Marina – To protect me from the trauma!

Marika – But how ...

Marina – According to my mother, we were in basinets next to each other at the maternity ward. She said the other baby was so ugly and frail ... She didn't think it could be hers ...

Carlota – Sounds like the wishful thinking of a deranged maid from Belarus…

Marina waits a few seconds for effect.

Marina – My mother kept my baby bracelet so she went and checked. It says Marika, not Marina.

The phone rings.

Carlota – Well, what are you waiting for ...? Answer it!

Marina – Marika Swindlemore von Hustlestein speaking. I can't hear you very well ... Ah yes, hello Mr Stonedef …

Carlota, furiously tears the handset away from Marina.

Carlota – Yes Frank ... No, not yet, I ... Oh really? Very well, I'll let her know immediately and I'll call you right back ...

She hangs up.

Carlota – That was Frank ... Asking for an answer to his marriage proposal. He can't wait any longer. He has to go back to California to receive last chance, life-saving treatment.

Marina —But I couldn't care less about your marriage projects! I've been cheated since birth! I am the baroness!

Carlota – Whoa there, girl. There's only one baroness here, and that's me.

Marina – But it's my birthright! The manor will be mine when you die!

Marika – Right now you're just a maid from Belarus…

Marina – You should be the maid! That's your birthright!

Marika's face falls apart.

Carlota – Let's all calm down, please ...

Marina – You're right ... Let's forget the titles and the estate. I just found a mother, after all ...

She runs into Carlota's arms, who doesn't know what to do.

Carlota – There, there ... In any case my poor girl ...

Marika – Could you please not call her your girl?

Carlota – The coffers are empty, Marina. Without this marriage, we won't even have enough to pay the maid, or anyone else for that matter. We only have this manor that's fallen into disrepair and a few family portraits.

Marina – In that case, I'll marry the billionaire. After all, he's only getting married for the title. He won't care or see who he's marrying. Not that he'd be worse off with me, anyway.

Marika and Marina stare at each other defiantly. Carlota steps in between them.

Carlota – Give us a minute please, Marina. We'll continue this discussion shortly.

Marina – Very well ... But I warn you, I won't be shortchanged.

The maid leaves.

Marika – It's a nightmare ...

Carlota – That's why it's important that you accept Mr Stonedef's proposal immediately.

Marika – Do you really think that's the most urgent right now?

Carlota – If you don't, we'll lose the goose that lays the golden eggs! We'll be flat broke.

Marika – And I may never get to be a baroness ...

Carlota – Who would want you if it turns out you don't have any blue blood? There won't be any redeeming feature to your ugly looks ... Nor any compensation ... *(Marika is crushed)* Don't worry. You'll still be my daughter no matter what. The flesh of my flesh. This wench could never be a baroness ... even if she is my biological daughter.

Marika – But what about Frank?

Carlota – You have to marry him right away, before he realises you're not the one he thinks you are ... Because then it will be too late.

Marika – You're right ...

Carlota – You should call him right away to tell him you accept his proposal.

Marika – And then?

Carlota – You elope to Las Vegas for a quickie ceremony. And you do the honeymoon on the way back.

Marika – And the maid?

Carlota – I'll take care of the maid while you're away ...

Marika – Very well. I'm off ... I hereby sacrifice myself for the Swindlemore name and manor.

Carlota – That's the spirit! ... True blood doesn't lie! I recognise in you the chivalrous and noble spirit that the Swindlemore von Hustlesteins have shown throughout history.

Marika – All is fair in love as in war!

They leave.

Black.

Act 2

Carlota is cleaning the room dressed in a French maid's outfit. Marina, dressed Sloane Ranger style, is reading a copy of Hello! *with a member of the royal family on the cover.*

Carlota – I'll say ... I hadn't realised how much chores were exhausting ...

Marina – That's nothing, wait until you start on the windows. It's impossible to get rid of all the streaks. But I'll give you a tip if you want ...

Carlota – Sure ...

Marina – Vinegar. Nothing better for cleaning glass.

Carlota – Not better than giving me a hand, surely?

Marina – Can't you see I'm busy reading! If I want to act in a manner befitting my rank, I have a lot of catching up to do. Especially regarding the comings and goings of the royal family. I didn't know these people's lives were so complicated.

Carlota – You have no idea ...

Marina – And all those double-barreled names. I thought the woke crowd had gotten rid of them.

Carlota – Thankfully we still have a few privileges left … I can give you a few tips too, if you want ...

Marina – Oh yes?

Carlota – How to get free accommodation, for example. When you're staying in the middle of nowhere, go and knock on the door of the local manor. It's going to be a cousin. There's always a guest room waiting for you.

Marina – I see ... Like a really posh AirBnB.

Carlota – Yes, exactly like that, but without central heating.

Marina – So you're all cousins, then ...?

Carlota – Yes ...

Marina – That explains this degenerate look you all have ... Speaking of which, have you heard from your daughter at all? I mean, from Marika ...

Carlota – Unfortunately not ... They have a policy restricting contact with friends and family for the first few weeks.

Marina – Oh, I didn't know that.

Carlota – But she'll come home eventually ...

Marina – This is all so very exhausting, I'm going to take a bath to try and relax a little.

Carlota – I understand ...

Marina *(about to leave)* – When you're done with the dusting, can you tackle the silverware? Not to be rude or anything, but this house was a pigsty when I arrived ...

Carlota – Hang on, I'm not your maid you know ...

Marina – Why would I need a maid when I have a mother?

Marina leaves.

Carlota – I guess I'll start on the windows then ...

Frank and Marika enter. Marika is carrying two suitcases. She is dressed differently and appears more radiant, having reclaimed her femininity. Frank also looks much healthier and is dressed in more cheerful clothes.

Carlota – Well, hello there children! You should have let me know you were coming today! I would have prepared your room ...

Marika – Mother? What is happening?

Carlota – How do you mean?

Marika – Don't tell me you're doing chores!

Carlota – Oh, that ... Don't worry about it dear, I'll explain later ...

Frank – Good afternoon, Madam Baroness.

Carlota – And how are you, my dear son?

Frank – Better. Much better ...

Carlota *(not overjoyed)* – Oh yes ... I see marriage becomes you.

Frank – My headaches have almost entirely disappeared. And sometimes I even feel like I have flashes of lucidity…

Carlota – You know what they say. Love is blind and marriage is an eye opener ... Tell me, when you say you're much better, do you mean ... you're not at death's door anymore?

Frank – It almost sounds like you'd be disappointed ...

Carlota – You're teasing me ... Of course not!

Frank – We'll all doing to die one day, aren't we?

Carlota – Indeed, we are ...

Frank – Well, it looks like that day will come later than we thought, after all.

Carlota – But that's wonderful news! Isn't it, darling?

Marika – Yes, of course ...

Carlota – So, tell us about your honeymoon ... How was Las Vegas?

Marika – You haven't received our postcard?

Carlota – Oh no, not yet. But you know, from the US it can take a while ...

Marika – In the end we got married in Blackpool in a registry office.

Frank – After our honeymoon, to comply with the 28 days notice required by the registry office.

Carlota – Oh, that's nice too ... Lancashire can be just as exotic as California. Did you have nice weather?

Marika – It rained for three weeks. We barely left our room at the Travelodge. *(Marika leans lovingly into Frank)* I don't regret not going to Las Vegas...

Frank – Me neither. Apparently, the Lancashire weather worked wonders, even better than the experimental treatment I was to receive in this US clinic.

Carlota – I can see that ...

Frank – Frank even took me to the Blackpool casino once.

Carlota – You don't say ...

Marika looks at Frank with a loving, knowing look.

Marika – But why go to the casino when you already hit the jackpot in bed ...

Frank *(lovingly)* – I think I played my cards right.

Carlota – Well ... Let's hope the odds will turn out in our favour…

Frank – I'll leave you two to talk for a bit. You must have a lot to say to each other. Mother-daughter talk and all that ... I'll go and freshen up a bit.

Carlota – I'll come with you ...

Frank – Don't worry, I can manage on my own ...

Carlota – You already know the layout of the manor, don't you?

Frank – And it's sort of mine too now, isn't it?

Carlota – Er, yes ...

Frank – I'll see you later, my love ... Can you get my suitcase delivered to my room?

Marika – I'll see you later, darling ...

Carlota looks at her daughter, worried. Once again Frank stumbles against the table on his way out, knocking over the vase.

Carlota – Well, well, well ... It looks like you managed to survive this ordeal after all ...

Marika – Yes, it's not as bad as I thought it would be ... I have to admit that I even take some pleasure in ...

Carlota – I'll thank you for sparing me the details of your wedding night ... You can tell me everything this winter around the fire. But we have more urgent business to discuss…

Marika – Business?

Carlota – Don't tell me you've already forgotten the unusual context of this love marriage?

Marika – No, of course not ...

Carlota – Because I was waiting for the return of the prodigal son-in-law to pay a few bills ... If we don't pay the People's Credit Union they'll foreclose on Swindlemore Hall!

Marika – We bank with the People's Credit Union?

Carlota – Alas, they're the only ones who will still take our business after the Rothschild Bank closed our account ... And if you think that's bad, if we can't find some dosh very quickly, we'll be making weekly calls at the food bank.

Marika – I'll talk to Frank, I promise ...

Carlota – Very well ... Come here then my dear ...

They hug for a bit.

Marina – And the maid?

Carlota – That's the second problem we need to solve ... I've done everything to manage her expectations. But she's starting to feel very much at home.

Marika – So you haven't fired her?

Carlota – She claims to be part of the family, you see ... And as you can tell by my clothes, I've had to make some compromises ... And when she finds out that ...

Just then Marina enters, followed by Frank.

Marina *(furious)* – Mr Stonedef just shared his wedding news ... You told me your daughter was in a drug rehab clinic!

Marika – You told her what?

Carlota – I had to tell her something.

Marina – So that's what it was all about? All your little lies and your sudden friendship… To give this ambitious bastard enough time to screw me over ...?

Carlota – Please, let's not get carried away ...

Frank – I have to say, Baroness, I can't believe what I'm hearing ... Are you confirming your maid's statements?

Marina – Oi, I'm not the maid!

Frank – I mean ... your biological daughter. But that's heinous! How can you use your own child as a servant?

Marika – Oh please, she's hardly Cinderella ...

Frank – As for me, I'm sure you can understand how I feel shortchanged ... I thought I was marrying a future baroness ...

Marina – And he ends up with a bastard child.

Marika – You're the bastard!

The two women are ready for a fist fight.

Carlota – Please ... Ladies ... Show a little dignity ... One of you is a blue-blood ...

Marina and Marika step away from each other. Marina starts walking towards Frank.

Marina – I am the baroness's daughter! You should have married me! *(She moves closer to Frank to flirt with him)* And believe you me, you wouldn't have been shortchanged in bed ...

Marika – How would you know, slag.

Carlota – Let's try and keep a level head, or we might say things we regret later.

Frank – Regardless, given these new elements, I wonder if it wouldn't be in my best interest to seek a divorce.

Carlota – Please don't, dearest! There's surely a way to resolve this small misunderstanding ...

Frank – A small misunderstanding? That's what it is to you…? I don't even know who I married anymore. The woman who said yes, or the one who will one day become Baroness Swindlemore?

Carlota – So, I've been thinking about this because I thought it might cause some tension ...

Marina – No kidding ...

Carlota – Here's what I propose ... Frank just married Marika. He'll keep his wife, who will one day become Baroness Swindlemore.

Marina – What about me?

Carlota – As compensation, Marina will inherit the manor and all its contents when I die.

Marika – I only get the title…? That's it…?

Carlota – Are you saying you'd prefer material belongings over the prestige of a name like ours?

Marika – No, of course not, but ...

Carlota – And many nobles inherited their blue-blood through maidservants, you know. A nationwide genetic test would likely reveal most of the maids are our cousins.

Marina, skeptical, nods her chin towards Frank and Marika.

Marina – What if they have children? They would have a claim to the estate ...

Carlota – Of course, Marika would be exempt from performing her wifely duties to avoid the legal inconvenience of any offspring. Also as a kindness to these poor children.

Marika – Wifely duties? From what I recall of our wedding night, it sure didn't look like it was a chore for my husband ...

Marina – Oh really?

The tension builds again between the two women.

Carlota – Right, so are things clear for everyone? What do you think Frank?

Marina – So I'll never be a baroness?

Marika – You get the manor, what are you complaining about?

Carlota – And you can still be Baroness Consort.

Marina – The baroness concert?

Carlota – Baroness Consort! Like Camilla will be Queen Consort to Prince Charles when he becomes King. You don't actually have the title, but you're part of the family. And should my daughter die, you'll be the baroness.

Marika – Charming.

Carlota – As for Mr Stonedef, he's not interested in my daughter's dowry anyway. He's a billionaire. He just wanted to marry a woman from a good family. And from that point of view, he got more than what he bargained for ...

Marina – More like bargain basement ...

Carlota *(to Marina)* – I'll treat you like my second daughter and Marika will consider you her sister ...

Marina – The Sisterhood of the Lying Pants ...

Carlota – What do you think, Frank?

Frank – And who will I perform my… marital duties with? I am married, after all ... This gives me certain privileges. It's bad enough to find out my wife isn't actually a baroness, on top of her not being the maiden I was led to believe, but I draw the line at celibacy!

Carlota – You can always sleep with the maid. That's probably what would have happened eventually anyway, like it does in all good comedies ...

Marika – Hey, I didn't agree to this!

Marina – Me neither!

Carlota – Oh don't be such prudes! We'll be one of those blended families ... it's very woke ...

Marina – Mmm ...

Frank – And who will do the chores?

Marina – Not me!

Carlota – So we need to hire a maid ... But Frank is rich, isn't he? And now he's the man of the family ... He'll provide for the needs of the entire family!

Frank – Yes, well, real estate isn't doing too well at the moment ... Even in California ...

Carlota – We just found out you weren't at death's door anymore, don't tell me we're now going to find out you're skint!

Frank – Unfortunately, that's exactly it, Mother ... But the most important thing in a marriage is the love between two people, isn't that right ...?

Carlota is about to faint.

Carlota – I'm not feeling well at all ...

Marika – Excuse us for a moment ...

The baroness leaves with her daughter. Along with Marina, Frank removes his glasses and they fall in each other's arms. We understand they are in it together.

Frank – It's done!

Marina – Life of Riley, here we come!

Frank – And how, Baroness Consort!

They kiss.

Marina – The bad news is that while you were away I found out they were defaulting on their loans and that the manor was the collateral.

Frank – Don't tell me I married this freak for nothing?

Marina – Sounds like the wedding night wasn't too much of a chore.

Frank – Are you kidding ... Have you seen that toad?

Marina – That's not what she said earlier ...

Frank – At least we still have the paintings ...

Marina – They must be worth a pretty penny ...

She goes to look at a painting close up but it falls off the wall.

Marina – Shit. Help me put it back up ...

Frank comes closer. As he picks up the painting, Marina looks on the back.

Marina – What's that?

Frank – What?

Marina – There's something written there ...

Frank – Maybe it's very valuable ... It happens you know, sometimes a painting by a nobody is eventually found to be by Michelangelo or Leonardo.

Marina – Leonardo? The actor or the football player?

Frank – Leonardo, the artist! Never mind, what does it say?

Marina looks closer.

Marina – I can't read it ... I don't have my glasses ... Have a look, you have better eyes than me ...

Frank reads the inscription.

Frank – Made in China ...

Marina – Made in China?

Frank – They're fakes.

Marina – No? Are you sure?

Frank – I don't think that at in olden times noblemen got their family portraits done in the People's Republic of China! *(A beat)* Do you know what that means? I married this end-of-race wench for fake paintings!

They are both deflated for a moment.

Marina – There's a few pieces of furniture ... But that won't get us very far ...

Frank – I don't believe it ...

Marina – We've been had ...

Frank – Yeah ... We've been double-crossed ...

Marina – But if these portraits are fakes, then ...

Frank – The Baroness's title might be too ...

Marina – No?

Frank pulls out his smartphone.

Frank – Hang on ... Let me google it ... Baroness of Swindlemore ... No way ... Look at this ...

He shows the smartphone screen to Marina.

Marina – No ...

Frank – Swindlemore von Hustlestein ... We should have known ...

Marina – We should have asked to see their letters patent ...

Frank – You can't trust anyone nowadays ...

Marina – Tell me about it ...

Frank – How come her daughter never tried to google herself?

Marina – Because these people still live in the Middle Ages! And the daughter is just out of private school! I bet her mother still has parental control on her internet access ...

Frank – So what do we do?

Marina – We hightail it! There's a few pieces of jewellery in the old crone's bedroom, upstairs. I'll grab them and we skip town before these two mythomaniacs come back.

Frank – I haven't even unpacked my suitcase, we can be out of here in minutes.

Marina leaves. As he waits, Frank uses his smartphone to find out more details about Carlota.

Frank – Look at that ... Wow ... She sure was a looker in her day ...

He is surprised when Carlota and Marika return.

Carlota – Are you seeing what I'm seeing?

Marika – But Frank, you're not blind?

Frank – Well, I mean ... I can see! It's a miracle!

Marina returns and calls out to Frank before she sees the two women.

Marina – Franky? We're good, I've got the jewellery, I hope they're not fakes like the rest ...

Frank moves towards Marina, arms stretched out to continue the pretense.

Frank – I can finally see you, my darling wife!

Marika – I'm your wife ...

Frank *(disappointed)* – Really ...? I'm not sure if it's really a miracle after all ...

Carlota – Go on ... You really take us for imbeciles ... So you were in it together from the beginning, is that it?

Marika – You're a couple of conmen?

Frank – Conmen ... Let's not exaggerate ...

Carlota – So you're neither blind nor a billionaire ... And this tramp isn't my biological daughter ...

Marina – Hey, watch it Baroness, or the tramp'll give you something to remember her by…

Carlota – And you did all that to convince us to agree to a marriage as soon as possible!

Marika – With the sole intention of taking everything from us!

Carlota – I can't believe it ...

Frank – Ok ... So now that everything is out in the open, what do we do?

Carlota – What do we do? I'll spell it out for you. You two, you get the hell out of here! And I'll press charges.

Frank – Hang on a minute. Ok, I'm neither blind nor a billionaire. But last time I checked that wasn't a crime. And now, whether you like it or not, I'm your son-in-law!

Marina – He's right, actually. And you were happy enough to marry your daughter to a blind man with a terminal illness to get his inheritance, so get off your high horse!

Carlota – You, the maid, no one asked you.

Marina – First off, I've never been a maid. And second, you're a dirty liar! The manor is about to be repossessed and the family portraits are fakes!

Marika – Fakes?

Carlota *(embarrassed)* – That's ridiculous ...

Marina – Is it?

Carlota – Obviously these people don't know anything about art. Fakes! You're one to talk ... I bet you've not even from Belarus ...

Frank – She's not the only one lying, isn't she, Baroness…?

Marika – Pardon?

Frank *(to Carlota)* – You haven't told us the whole truth about your origins, have you ...

Carlota *(embarrassed)* – Me?

Frank – Your husband was a porn star. And you met him on set! Wikipedia has the whole story right here ...

Carlota – I asked them multiple times to take down this article ...

Marika – I thought Daddy was a dressage champion and that he died falling off a horse?

Frank – That's one way of putting it ... She just conveniently forgot to tell you who he was mounting ...

Marina – And that the context in which this ride took place ...

Frank – All you need to know is that it was an X-rated version of The Magnificent Seven.

Carlota – It had a strong plot, I'll have you know ...

Marina – I'm sure ... No doubt the residuals you earned from these plot-driven films paid for this manor.

Frank – Earning yourself some desperately needed respectability in the process…

Marika – Oh my God ... Please, someone tell me this isn't true! I thought I had hit rock bottom when I found out I was the daughter of a maid from Belarus… So, wait ... Who are my parents? And who am I?

Marina – Don't worry, you really are your mother's daughter ... As for your father, he signed the birth certificate with an X, so who knows ...

Frank *(tapping on his smartphone)* – You might have been conceived during the shooting of a cult classic such as ... *(showing the screen to Marika) My Fair Ladies* ... A masterpiece of filmmaking in which Carlota bears the title of Baroness for the first time.

Marina – ... and bares it all for the entirety of the film.

Carlota – I came a hair's width to winning a Shafta award for that one ...

Frank – So you can see how I too, might think I have been misled about the pedigree of my guide dog.

The baroness is embarrassed.

Marika – Say something, mother ...

Carlota – It's true, I may have rewritten a small part of our family history ...

Marika – So you're not Baroness Swindlemore von Hustlestein ... But what about the family portraits?

Carlota – They are absolutely genuine, I promise. Well, I mean, the ones that were used to make these copies ... Only ... They are not our family ...

Marika – This is a nightmare ...

Carlota – Look at the bright side, you really are my daughter!

Marika – The daughter of a whore! I'm overjoyed ...

Carlota – Actually, I prefer the term sex performer ...

Marika – I'm sorry, I wouldn't want to sound disrespectful.

Carlota – I even qualified for a SAG membership, I'll have you know!

Marika *(ironically)* – You're right, this isn't the 18th century anymore. Female actors aren't automatically assumed to be prostitutes ...

Marina – Alright, are you both about done with this touching heart-to-heart?

Carlota – Isn't there a middle ground? A good compromise is better than a nasty divorce.

Marika – A middle ground?

Carlota – The truth is that we can't even afford to hire a maid. And since we can't count on our fake nobility to find you an ideal husband ...

Frank – Especially since your daughter is already married ... Just a reminder ...

Carlota – You see, darling, we have to find a compromise ...

Marika – We can't even sell those family portraits. They're copies…! They're worthless!

Frank – We would rent out the manor to porn film directors? Madam Baroness here must still have contacts.

Carlota – What would our friends say ... And the vicar ... I'm thinking something more appropriate ... I don't know ... A classical music festival, for example!

Marina – But of course ... We can even ask the council for funds, maybe even the EU ...

Carlota – Making classical music available to the disadvantaged and underprivileged is very much in keeping with our woke times.

Marina – But of course ... A classical music concert accessible to the culturally disabled. Whatever next?

Frank – Ok, how about a themed AirBnB? People love manors and a baroness will make it look more authentic.

Marika – My husband and I could be the managers. And Marina could do the housekeeping ...

Marina – Hey, Frank is my man, understood!

Marika – Maybe, but he's my husband. And now that I know that Mr Stonedef isn't blind ... And given I find him rather attractive ... And that I know how skilled he is with his hands ...

Marika and Marina are about to fight. Frank steps in and separates them.

Carlota – Come now, there's surely a compromise here as well. People of our class always find a solution, don't we?

Marika – And by class you mean conmen?

Carlota – Yes, that too ...

Black

Epilogue

Marika, wearing a French maid's outfit, is dusting using a feather duster. The other three are sat in comfortable seats, drinking tea. The atmosphere is that of high-society.

Marina – May I have another cup please ...

Marika pours her tea clumsily and with clenched teeth.

Carlota – Don't worry my dear, tomorrow it will be your turn to be Baroness.

Frank – And her turn to be the maid.

Carlota – We said every other day ...

Frank – My dear mother-in-law, I think we just invented the concept of marriage in shifts.

Carlota – And that of rotating democracy.

Frank – No need to cheat on the Mrs with the help like in a bad boulevard comedy: I just have to wait until tomorrow when the maid becomes my wife!

Carlota – And your wife, the maid.

Frank – A dream come true.

Carlota – You were right after all, my dear son ... This is the life of Riley ... Isn't it, ladies?

Marika and Marina exchange looks.

Marina – Dearest Baroness sister wife, sometimes I wonder if we aren't just the butts of an elaborate family joke ...

Carlota – Speaking of families, don't forget that Christmas is coming up fast.

Frank – I am really looking forward to spending the holidays with family for the first time.

Carlota – There's nothing like family. *(A beat)* Speaking of which, since we're all together, I want to take this opportunity to share some news, Frank.

Frank – Oh yes? What is it?

Carlota – There will be a new addition to the family ...

Frank – A baby for Christmas? But that's wonderful! Who's the mother?

Marika and Marina exchange a hateful look, before turning towards Carlota, suspiciously. Carlota looks barely embarrassed.

Carlota – Another miracle, apparently ...

Frank *(to lighten the atmosphere)* – How about some music?

Carlota – Perfect! But only classical music, please.

Frank – Of course, I wouldn't dream of playing anything else.

Carlota – Music to my ears.

Frank uses a remote control to start a classical music track chosen by the production team (for example, Ode to Joy).

While the volume of the music increases, the lights dim on this touching portrait of family bliss.

Black.

The end.

July 2022

www.ingramcontent.com/pod-product-compliance
Lightning Source LLC
La Vergne TN
LVHW010122170826
845678LV00012B/2550
9782377057955